Get Your Tutti-Frutti Punch!

"No fair!" said Missy. "You're stealing my business."

"It's a free country." Stephanie shrugged.

"But there's already one lemonade stand on this block," Missy protested.

"This happens to be tutti-frutti punch," Stephanie replied indignantly.

A car slowed down as it drove past. "Get your fresh lemonade!" Missy shouted.

"Try my tutti-frutti punch! It's made with six different fruit juices!"

The man looked at Missy's stand and then at Stephanie's. Stephanie flashed her sickening-sweet smile. The red-and-white awning flapped invitingly.

"I think I'll try the punch," the man said finally.

Missy wanted to scream. Stephanie Cook, Miss Perfect, had done it again.

A Dog Named Baby

by **Molly Albright**

illustrated by **Dee deRosa**

Troll

A Dog Named Baby

CHAPTER

1

"**H**ey, wait for me!" yelled Melissa Fremont. She clutched her book bag tightly and raced toward the school bus.

Her friends, Emily Green and Wilhelmina Wagnalls, leaned out of one of the windows at the back of the bus. "Hurry up, Missy," called Emily. "You don't want to get stuck at school, do you?"

Missy grinned. "No way!" she shouted. She managed to reach the bus just as the door was closing.

As she stomped up the steps, she caught Mr. Covey, the bus driver, glaring at her. "You're lucky you made it," he growled. Mr. Covey was the grouchiest bus driver in Indianapolis. Anytime he felt the students were getting too noisy, he'd pull the bus off the road, turn off the engine, and wait until there was total silence. One morning he stopped for half an hour. The bus was late to school, and everyone got tardy slips.

Missy brushed her mop of curly red hair out of her eyes and smiled weakly. "Sorry, Mr. Covey," she said. "I was talking to our teacher about our class project. We've been studying American history all year, so we're going to Washington, D.C.—if we can raise the money."

Mr. Covey raised his eyebrows.

"Missy had this great idea," Wilhelmina (Willie, for short) told him. "She suggested that we have a class competition to see which student can earn the most money to help pay for the trip."

Emily added excitedly, "And Ms. Van Sickel told us that whatever money *we* earn will be matched by people who own stores and businesses here in Indianapolis."

Mr. Covey just grunted and glanced into his rearview mirror.

Missy made her way to the rear of the bus where the older kids always sat. "Look out, D.C.! Here we come," shouted Adam Ramirez. He tossed his baseball cap into the air and gave a loud cheer.

"Hey, you kids, settle down back there," shouted Mr. Covey as he backed the bus into the street.

Missy's classmate and neighbor, Stephanie Cook, folded her arms and shrugged. "I think the whole idea is stupid," she said. "Besides, what's so hard about raising a little money?"

"We can't use our allowance money, and we can't accept money from our parents," retorted Adam. "Give me a break!"

Stephanie just shook her head and tossed her long blond hair over her shoulder. Missy noticed that she was wearing a stylish new blue sweater that matched the color of her eyes. Stephanie was the best-dressed and best-looking girl in Missy's class, and she knew it. Missy's secret nickname for Stephanie was "Ms. Perfect."

Stephanie Cook was definitely *not* one of Missy's favorite people. She remembered how stuck-up and bossy Stephanie had acted when Missy first moved to Indianapolis from Cincinnati last September. Missy had been the "new girl" in school then, and Stephanie never let her forget it!

If it hadn't been for Baby, Missy never would have survived Stephanie and that horrible first week at Hills Point School. Baby was Missy's huge Old English sheepdog and her best friend. He was enormous now, but he had been just a tiny ball of fur when Missy chose him. The fact that she had chosen him made him special, like Missy, whose parents had chosen *her,* when she was a tiny baby waiting to be adopted.

Missy was very happy at Hills Point now, and she had made some good friends. Stephanie was still a pain, though. With enemies like Stephanie around, Missy knew she'd always need a best friend like Baby!

Missy's thoughts about Baby and Stephanie were interrupted by a low, rumbling sound. With a start, Missy realized the sounds were coming from her stomach. She put her hand on her stomach, hoping no one had heard it rumbling. She took a deep breath and waited. Finally, the rumbling stopped, and Missy breathed a sigh of relief. No one had heard her. No one, that is, except Stephanie.

"I thought I heard the sound of thunder," said Stephanie sweetly. "Did *you* hear it, Missy?"

Missy gritted her teeth and stared straight ahead. "Leave it to Stephanie," she thought. She made a mental note to add "Ms. Big Ears" to her list of nicknames for Stephanie.

Just then, Emily reached into her knapsack and pulled out a bag of cheese-flavored popcorn. "Anybody want some?" she asked. At the sight of it, Missy's stomach started to rumble again.

"Me," she said quickly. "I lost my salami sandwich this morning, so I didn't have any lunch. I'm starving."

"Salami?" sniffed Stephanie. "How disgusting."

"Salami is *not* disgusting," retorted Missy. "It's delicious. Besides, it's Baby's favorite, next to hard-boiled eggs."

"Oh, you and your big Baby," Stephanie said. "Everybody knows he'd eat *anything,* even greasy gross-out food like salami."

Missy felt her face grow warm with anger. She and Baby were two of a kind. If Stephanie insulted Baby, she was insulting Missy too!

Emily gave her a nudge. "Ignore her," she whispered. "She's just trying to pick a fight with you!"

Missy was about to defend Baby and his love of salami, but she decided to take Emily's advice instead. Arguing with Stephanie was like trying to peel an onion with gloves on. It got you nowhere fast!

In the last seat of the bus, Adam and Tommy Lawson started to whisper and snicker loudly.

"Oh, Missy," Adam sang out. "Look what we just

found." He dangled a small sandwich bag in the air.

"It's my salami sandwich!" Missy cried. "Where did you find it?"

"It was under my seat," Adam replied. "You must have dropped it out of your lunch bag."

Missy reached over to take the sandwich. Her stomach was rumbling like a freight train, and her mouth was beginning to water.

"Oh, no, you don't," said Adam. He snatched the sandwich away and tossed it toward the front of the bus. It hit a second grader on the back of the head.

"Ow," said the second grader. He threw the sandwich onto the floor and kicked it across the aisle.

"Give me back my sandwich," Missy yelled. She stood up in her seat, but Tommy grabbed the back of her jacket and pulled her back down.

"Let go of me, you creep!" Missy shouted.

In the front of the bus, her sandwich was getting kicked up and down the aisle like a mini-soccer ball. "Score!" shouted Andy Martin. The plastic sandwich bag ripped apart and the two pieces of bread flopped across the floor. Andy grabbed a slice of salami and sailed it across the bus like a Frisbee. "Nice toss!" yelled Tommy, who had caught it.

"Stop that!" Missy shouted. No one paid any attention.

"Keep it away from Missy!" shouted Adam.

Missy lunged at the salami and missed.

Mr. Covey pulled off the road and threw on the

brakes. "Okay, kids," he said. "I can sit here forever. I don't care *when* you get home." He switched off the engine.

The bus grew silent. Adam and Tommy started to snicker.

"I expect *total silence*," Mr. Covey roared.

Stephanie turned around and gave the boys a dirty look. "Shh," she said. "Do you want to sit here forever?" She turned back and folded her hands obediently on her lap.

When everything was quiet, Mr. Covey started up the bus, put his turn signal on, and began to pull back onto the road. There was a loud scream from the back of the bus. Mr. Covey stopped again.

"Gross!" screamed Stephanie. "Gross, gross, gross." She was standing in the aisle frantically flapping her sweater. A tattered piece of salami fell to the floor.

"You put that greasy old salami down my back on purpose!" she said to Adam.

"Who, me?" said Adam innocently. Everyone on the bus started to laugh.

Stephanie turned angrily to Missy, who was laughing too. "What's so funny?" she said. "If you hadn't lost your stupid sandwich, none of this would have happened."

Missy tried to wipe the grin off her face. "Sorry, Stephanie," she replied with a giggle.

Stephanie looked at Mr. Covey. He was sitting with his legs crossed and his arms folded. "Are you finished?" he asked.

Stephanie pursed her lips and sat down with a loud huff. Mr. Covey slowly drove on. By the time they got to Missy's street, the bus had been completely silent for ten whole blocks. Missy and the others who lived in the neighborhood started to gather up their things. Stephanie didn't budge. "This is our stop, Stephanie," Missy said finally.

"Don't you think I know that?" Stephanie replied. She threw her hair back and walked to the front of the bus. "I can't believe how immature *some* people are," she said haughtily. She stepped off the bus and carefully rearranged her sweater. Suddenly, a piece of salami came sailing out the window, followed by a piece of bread.

"Watch out!" Adam shouted. "Low-flying objects."

Before anyone had a chance to duck, Baby dashed around the corner and snatched the salami in midair. He swallowed it in one gulp. The kids on the bus burst into applause.

Missy ran over and gave Baby a big hug. "Good catch," she said. Baby licked her face appreciatively. Suddenly, he stopped and put his nose in the air. He looked over at Stephanie and barked. Stephanie took two steps back. Missy tried to grab Baby's collar, but she wasn't quick enough. Baby threw his paws on Stephanie's shoulders, knocking her to the ground. He rubbed his furry nose on her back and wagged his tail.

"Help!" shrieked Stephanie. "Get him off me."

Missy tugged on Baby's collar, trying not to laugh. "It's not his fault," she gulped. "He smells the salami." The kids on the school bus were hanging out the windows and laughing.

"Down, Baby!" Missy ordered.

But Baby grabbed the back of Stephanie's sweater and shook it furiously.

"Do something!" cried Stephanie. "He's ruining my new sweater!"

Missy gave another tug and Baby finally let go. "Bad dog," said Missy.

Stephanie stood up and brushed herself off as the school bus slowly pulled away. "I have never been so humiliated in my life," she said to Missy. "And it's *your* fault!"

Missy held on to Baby's collar tightly as she watched Stephanie stomp off across the street to her house. "Come on, Baby," she sighed. "I'm taking you home."

CHAPTER

2

It was Mr. Fremont's turn to cook dinner that night, and he made one of Missy's favorites—megaburgers with all the trimmings. Missy was so hungry, she was already chewing on her second inch-thick burger with fried onions and mushrooms before she brought up the subject of the class trip and the competition to her parents.

"Washington is quite a town," said Mr. Fremont as he helped himself to some potato salad. Missy's father was a viola player, and he'd recently been to Washington, D.C., on tour with the Indianapolis Symphony.

"What kinds of places will you be visiting?" asked Mrs. Fremont. She was a kindergarten teacher, so she cared about those things.

"The usual," Missy replied. "The monuments, the museums, the Mint, the White House." Missy thought for a few minutes. "Do you have any good ideas about how I can raise money?" she asked. "I was thinking about having a dog wash next Saturday."

"Great idea," said Mr. Fremont. "It's supposed to be a glorious spring day."

Missy picked up her dinner plate. "May I be excused?" she asked. "I want to go make some phone calls. I can think of at least eight people who own dogs."

Mrs. Fremont nodded and smiled. "Just don't forget about your homework," she said.

"It's okay, Mom," Missy replied. "I've already finished it."

Missy went to her room and started to make a list of possible customers.

Just then, the phone rang.

"Missy, telephone," called her mother. "It's Stephanie Cook."

"What does Ms. Perfect want now?" Missy groaned. She went to the kitchen and picked up the receiver. "Hello?"

"I'll have you know my new sweater is ruined," snapped Stephanie.

"I'm sorry," said Missy, "but Baby really couldn't help it."

"I got that sweater at Thimble Threads," Stephanie continued. "Not only was it new, it also happened to be my favorite. I think you should pay for it."

Missy didn't know what to say. Everything in Thimble Threads was really expensive. "How much did it cost?" she asked weakly.

"Forty dollars," Stephanie replied.

Missy gulped. Forty dollars! She didn't have anywhere *near* that amount of money. Besides, how was she ever going to raise money for the trip to Washington if she had to repay Stephanie?

"I'll see what I can do," Missy muttered. Stephanie slammed down the phone before Missy had a chance to say good-by.

Missy's mother was in the living room reading a magazine. "Mom," said Missy, "can I talk to you?" She explained her predicament. "Do I really have to pay for her sweater?" she asked.

Mrs. Fremont sighed. "I'm afraid so," she said. "You're responsible for Baby." Missy's mother smiled. "Why don't I take you to Thimble Threads after school tomorrow? If Stephanie's sweater is new, they'll probably have another one. I just hope it's the same color."

"But where am I going to get the money to pay for it?" Missy groaned.

"I guess your dad and I will have to lend it to you," said Mrs. Fremont.

Missy flopped down on the sofa next to her mother. "Thanks, Mom," she said. She reached over and scratched Baby behind the ears. "And no more tricks from you," she told him. "At this rate, I'll never win the competition."

A few days later at the bus stop Missy shoved a plastic bag from Thimble Threads into Stephanie's arms. "Here," she said. "A Fremont never goes back on her word."

Stephanie opened the bag. "Oh!" she said sweetly.

"Didn't I tell you? My mother fixed the sweater." She looked at Missy with a concerned expression. "You can always return it," she said.

"Thanks a *lot,* Stephanie," Missy fumed. She'd had to borrow the money from her mother to buy that sweater. Not only that, but the salesgirl had stamped "SALE—NO RETURN" on the receipt. Missy knew her mother was going to be furious with Stephanie when she found out.

Just then, Adam walked over to them. "Are either of you interested in buying any of my old comic books?" he asked. "I'm selling them to raise money for the trip."

"Do you have any *True Romance* comics?" asked Stephanie.

Adam made a face. "Are you crazy?" he said. "I don't read that junk." He smiled at Missy. "What about you, Missy?"

Adam had a nice smile. Missy wondered why she'd never noticed it before. She smiled back. "Sorry, Adam," she said. "I'm not interested in comics."

"How are you planning to earn money?" Adam asked her.

"I'm having a dog wash this Saturday," Missy replied. "Be sure to tell all the dog owners that you know."

"That's funny," interrupted Stephanie. "I'm having a car wash next Saturday. I can think of a lot more people who own cars."

Missy smiled as sweetly as she could. "I just hope you don't wear your baby-blue sweater on the job, Stephanie. Car grease is even tougher to get out than salami," she said. Then she took the bag from Thimble Threads and shoved it into her book bag. "Car wash," she snorted.

"Dog wash," Stephanie snickered.

Missy marched onto the bus. This competition was already turning into a lot more than she'd ever expected.

CHAPTER

3

That day at school, everyone was talking about the competition. Several of the students already had activities planned. Christine Coogan and Meredith Lilly were teaming up to sell peanut butter cookies. "It's Meredith's grandmother's recipe," Christine told the class. "No artificial ingredients."

David Holt was going to give bicycle tune-ups in front of his house, after school and on weekends.

"I hope everyone will tell their parents about my car wash," Stephanie announced.

Adam hooted. "*You're* washing cars?" he said.

"What's wrong with that?" Stephanie retorted. "It's a lot better than selling old comic books."

Ms. Van Sickel, their teacher, clapped her hands. "Please be seated, class," she said. "We have lots to do today."

Emily raised her hand. "You forgot to tell us

how long the competition is supposed to last," she said.

"How about three weeks?" Ms. Van Sickel suggested. "The trip is scheduled in five weeks. That should give us enough time to see how we're doing . . . and whether we'll need any school funds."

"Ms. Van Sickel," whined Ashley Woods, "I can't think of anything to do." Ashley had been a new girl in school, like Missy. Because all the other girls already knew one another, Missy had gotten stuck with Ashley when it came time to choose study buddies at the beginning of the year.

Ms. Van Sickel smiled. "Maybe you can do something with your study buddy," she suggested.

Missy quickly raised her hand. "But I'm having a dog wash," she said.

Ashley sneezed. "I'm allergic to dogs," she said.

"I know," said Missy, rolling her eyes. Ashley was allergic to just about everything!

Ms. Van Sickel gave Ashley a sympathetic look. "Sorry, Ashley," she said. "I'm afraid you're on your own."

Lawrence Shoemaker raised his hand. "I could use a partner for my project," he said.

Ashley turned up her nose. "Forget it," she said. The class began to laugh.

"That's enough," Ms. Van Sickel said in a loud, stern voice. "I'm sure Lawrence has a very good idea."

Poor Lawrence. With his thick glasses and short pants, he was the class joke. Missy felt really sorry for him sometimes.

As soon as the recess bell rang, Emily and Willie

ran over to Missy. "Guess what?" Emily said. "We think Lawrence has a crush on Ashley."

"Gross," said Missy. "Are you sure?"

"Why else would he ask her to share his project?" Willie replied.

Emily giggled. "I don't think Lawrence has washed his hair in two years," she said.

"Ashley and Lawrence," said Missy. "The perfect couple." She and Emily and Willie laughed all the way to the cafeteria.

That evening Missy stood in front of her bathroom mirror and bared her teeth.

"Practicing your Frankenstein face?" asked Mr. Fremont as he walked past.

Missy quickly stopped. "Dad," she said, looking into the mirror, "do my teeth look crooked to you?"

Mr. Fremont peered inside Missy's mouth. "Straight as arrows," he replied. "Why?"

"I think it would be neat to have braces," Missy said. "There are already seven people in our class who have them."

"Oh, really?" said Mr. Fremont.

"They get to miss school all the time for dentist's appointments, and they're allowed to drink as many milk shakes as they want."

"Is that so?" said Mr. Fremont. "Hmmm. Milk shakes, you say? Maybe we should look into this."

"Be serious, Dad," pleaded Missy. "Can't you see how crooked my teeth are becoming?"

"Not really," he answered.

Missy gave an exasperated sigh. "Never mind," she said.

"How are your dog-wash plans coming?" asked her father.

"Fine," said Missy. "I passed out fliers at school and put up a few posters. I should be getting lots of customers."

"I noticed that your friend Stephanie put up a sign in her driveway, advertising a car wash this Saturday. I thought maybe I'd take the car over."

"Dad!" said Missy. "She's *not* my friend. She's my competition!"

Mr. Fremont scratched his forehead. "But I thought all the money you raised was going into a big pile to get your class to Washington."

Missy shook her head. "But first it comes in little piles—and if Stephanie's pile is bigger than mine, she'll never let me forget it."

Her father grinned. "So, maybe I should take my dog to your dog wash."

Missy grinned back. "I'd call it a matter of family loyalty."

Mr. Fremont hugged his daughter. "How would you like an Old English sheepdog as your first customer?"

CHAPTER

4

Missy was up and ready to go early Saturday morning. As she pulled on her jeans, she glanced out her window. Across the street, Stephanie, dressed in a hot pink jumpsuit, was already busy organizing.

Missy could see that Stephanie had recruited two helpers: her younger sister, Denise, and Moose Munson, a high-school kid who lived down the block. Moose was a star football player and had muscles like watermelons.

"I should have known," groaned Missy. "Ms. Perfect would *never* risk getting her designer jumpsuit covered with gunk." With both Denise and Moose to help her, Stephanie definitely had a head start in the competition—a big one! Missy knew she'd better get a move on. " 'Morning, Mom, Dad," Missy shouted as she ran through the kitchen. She gulped down a glass of orange juice and shoved

Baby out the door. "Time to get going," she said.

Outside, Missy hooked up the garden hose. Then she brought out her bucket of supplies: dog shampoo, a comb and brush, and a stack of old towels. Next, she ran an extension cord from her bedroom window out to the front lawn and attached her hair dryer. Missy set up a folding chair for herself and spread out an old blanket for Baby. After she taped her poster to the front of the mailbox, she sat down in her chair and waited.

Across the street, Stephanie was giving orders to Moose. "Moose, do me one teeny-weeny favor and get the hose from the garage," she said sweetly. Moose obediently sprinted off to the garage. Stephanie waited on the front lawn and brushed her hair. Moose jogged out of the garage with the hose slung over his shoulder. "Put it over there," Stephanie directed.

A car pulled up in front of Missy's house. Missy quickly stood up. A man wearing a football jersey hopped out. "Is this the car wash?" he asked.

Missy hesitated. "No," she said finally, "the car wash is across the street."

The man turned around. "Oh, you're right," he said. "Say, isn't that Moose Munson over there?" He quickly got back into his car. "Thanks very much," he called out to Missy.

Missy sat down in her lawn chair with a sigh. Across the street, Moose was sponging down the man's car. Stephanie was showing Denise how to rinse off the suds with the hose. Missy looked

at Baby. "I hope we get a customer soon," she whispered.

Several minutes later another car pulled up. "Is this the dog wash?" asked a skinny woman with the thickest false eyelashes Missy had ever seen.

"Yes," Missy said with a sigh of relief. At last!

The woman opened the back door of her car, and five tiny chihuahuas tumbled out. They were all wearing matching sweaters, each embroidered with a different name. Two of the dogs started to growl at each other. "Topper, Snappy, settle down," said the woman. The dogs pranced anxiously until each one was hooked up to a rhinestone leash.

The woman gathered her charges together and wobbled across the lawn in a tight green skirt and black heels. "Where would you like them?" she asked.

Baby stood up and sniffed the chihuahuas suspiciously. The oldest one, who had gray chin whiskers, growled back.

Missy noticed a second car pulling into Stephanie's driveway.

"You can leave all five of them in the back yard until I'm ready to wash them," Missy told her. "I wouldn't want them to run off."

The woman raised her penciled eyebrows. "I should hope not," she said. "These are my babies." The lady led the dogs to the back yard and then turned to go. "Is one hour enough time?"

"Certainly," Missy replied.

The woman teetered back across the lawn and drove off.

Missy looked down at the cluster of tiny dogs.

The dog with the hairy gray chin, Topper, appeared to be in charge. Missy carefully led him to the front yard and got started.

"Nice doggie," said Missy. Topper growled. Missy glanced up and noticed Stephanie watching her. Missy pointed to the back yard. "Five dogs!" she exclaimed. "Can you believe it!"

Stephanie abruptly turned around and started talking to Moose, who was furiously polishing the chrome on a customer's car.

Missy wet Topper down with the garden hose and then dumped a capful of dog shampoo onto his back. Baby put his tail between his legs and whimpered.

"Relax," said Missy. "I'm washing other people's dogs, not you!"

Missy quickly rinsed Topper off and dried him with the hair dryer. "These little dogs are a cinch," she said loudly. "*Much* easier than *cars*."

Across the street, Moose and Denise were working on another car. Stephanie was daintily cutting up an old T-shirt to use as polishing cloths. Missy rolled her eyes. Only Stephanie would use scissors to *cut* up a T-shirt instead of *tearing* it up, like a normal person!

"Hi, Missy," said Amy Flanders. "I've brought Angus over for a bath." Amy was a classmate of Missy's. She'd just gotten braces last Friday.

Angus, a black Labrador, barked a greeting to Baby and tugged impatiently on his leash. Baby barked back and wagged his tail. The two dogs were good friends. "Put him in the back yard with the chihuahuas," Missy said.

"How's business?" asked Amy as she tugged on Angus's leash.

"Good so far," Missy replied. "I've had six customers, including Angus." She glanced across the street at Stephanie.

"My mom's over there getting her car washed," Amy explained. "Stephanie's had six customers too."

"She has?" said Missy. Another car pulled into Stephanie's driveway.

"Seven," said Amy. She pulled a small mirror out of her back pocket and checked her braces for food particles. "I'll be back in a while," she said. "I'm going over to see Stephanie."

Missy watched Amy cross the street and quickly returned to work. She managed to finish the chihuahuas just as the skinny woman pulled up.

"You did a lovely job," said the woman, reaching into her purse. "How long will you be here?"

"Just this afternoon," Missy replied.

The woman glanced at her watch. "I'll try to get some of my friends over," she promised.

"Great," said Missy. "I can use all the customers you send me."

By mid-afternoon, Missy's back yard was full of dogs waiting to be washed. Stephanie's driveway looked pretty full too.

Missy was just finishing a springer spaniel named Clover when Stephanie walked over. "You seem really busy," Stephanie said.

"Swamped," Missy replied. "Couldn't be busier."

Stephanie peered into the back yard. "How many customers do you have left?" she asked.

Missy shrugged. "Lots," she replied. She narrowed her eyes. "How about you?"

"The same," said Stephanie.

Missy put her hair dryer down for a minute. "By the way, Stephanie," she said. "How did you get Moose Munson to help you out?"

Stephanie smiled. "My mother is going to bake him one of her famous triple chocolate cakes. Moose is a real chocolate freak."

"Missy, telephone," called Mrs. Fremont. "It's Emily."

Missy hesitated. She didn't really want to leave Stephanie alone in her yard.

Stephanie must have read Missy's mind. "Go ahead. I'll be glad to watch your customers for a few minutes. My helpers have everything under control across the street."

Missy quickly ran inside. "Hi, Emily," she said. "What's up?" There was no reply. "Hello? Hello?" Missy repeated. She held the receiver out and looked at it. "She must have hung up."

Missy found Stephanie in the back yard petting the dogs. "I see you have four customers left," Stephanie said. "That makes us *almost* even. I have three."

"Oh, really?" said Missy, trying not to sound triumphant.

Stephanie straightened up. "Gotta go," she said. "Moose and Denise can't handle things forever."

"Right," said Missy. She quickly brought a golden retriever named Bravo to the front yard and returned to work. Two more cars had already lined up in Stephanie's driveway.

Missy turned on the hose and ran to Bravo. But when she picked up the hose, no water came out. "Baby," she called, turning around. "Are you sitting on the hose?" But Baby was nowhere near the hose, and Missy could see why. A big gush of water was spurting out of the middle, near Baby's blanket. Baby was running away, yelping.

"Uh-oh," said Missy. "We're in big trouble."

Missy put Bravo in the back yard and went inside the house. "Dad," she called, "I think our hose has sprung a leak."

She could hear Mr. Fremont practicing his viola down in the basement. "Be right there," he said.

Two more customers were waiting for Missy when she walked back outside. "I'll be with you in just a minute," Missy told them.

Mr. Fremont examined the hose carefully.

"Can it be fixed?" Missy asked anxiously.

Mr. Fremont frowned. "I'm not sure," he replied. "This hose looks like it's been pierced with a sharp object."

Missy was shocked. "You mean with a knife?" she said.

Mr. Fremont pointed to the hole. "This is a pretty big gash," he said. "I can't imagine how else it got here."

Missy glanced across the street. Was it possible? Missy remembered seeing Stephanie cutting up that T-shirt with her scissors earlier. Now Stephanie was hard at work supervising Denise, who was polishing a big red car.

"Are you going to be able to give Hobo a bath?" Andy Martin interrupted.

Missy looked at her father.

"Sorry, Missy," he said. "I need to make a trip to the hardware store for a patch if you want the hose fixed. And it's going to take a couple of hours for the patch to dry."

Missy took a deep breath and then marched across the street to Stephanie's.

"What are you doing here?" asked Stephanie.

"While I was inside on the phone, a hole appeared in our garden hose," Missy stated.

"So?"

"*So,* I'd like to know how it got there!"

Stephanie shrugged. "How should I know?" she said. "Maybe Baby did it."

Missy frowned. On the other side of the driveway, Denise stopped what she was doing and stared at Stephanie.

"Mind your own business, Denise!" Stephanie yelled.

Denise quickly bent down and started scrubbing again.

"Baby has never chewed anything in his life," Missy said.

Stephanie shrugged again. "If I found a hole in my garden hose right where the dog was sitting, I'd have my suspicions."

"Never mind, then," sighed Missy. She was halfway across the street when it hit her. "Wait a minute," she said as she spun around. "How did *you* know where the hole was?"

Stephanie looked at her, surprised.

Missy's eyes narrowed. "I knew it!" she said. "You had *guilty* written all over your face."

Stephanie put her hands on her hips. "You can't prove anything," she said.

"Oh, yeah?" Missy replied. "You'd better watch out from now on, Stephanie," she said. "This means war."

CHAPTER

5

"**D**ad," said Missy, "do you have to practice your viola tonight?"

Mr. Fremont took a bite of his pork chop. "What did you have in mind?" he asked.

It had been three days since Missy's dog wash. She had decided to give it up after a neighbor's cat strayed into the yard. All the dogs went wild, even Baby. Missy decided that dog washing was a risky business. But she was sick of hearing Stephanie brag about her millions of customers. There was no way she was going to let Stephanie beat her.

"I was thinking of starting a lemonade stand," Missy said.

"I hope you're not planning to ask your father to build it," Mrs. Fremont laughed.

Mr. Fremont put down his napkin. "Wait a minute, Pat! I'm a perfectly good carpenter!" he said.

"What about those bookshelves you built when we were first married?" teased Mrs. Fremont.

"They should never have fallen down," insisted Mr. Fremont. "The guy at the hardware store sold me the wrong brackets."

Missy cleared her throat. "Mom, Dad, do you mind?"

Mr. Fremont turned to his daughter. "I thought you weren't allowed to have any help from your parents," he said.

"They just can't give us *money*," Missy replied. She paused. "Please, Dad? Will you help me build it?"

Mr. Fremont smiled. "I suppose the old viola can wait one more night," he said. "How soon do you want to get started?"

Twenty minutes later Mr. Fremont, Missy, and Baby were standing in the Fremonts' garage. "Now, where did I put that hammer?" said Mr. Fremont.

"You're holding it." Missy grinned.

Mr. Fremont looked down. "By golly, you're right!" he exclaimed.

Mr. Fremont dragged several scraps of lumber to the middle of the garage and leaned them against an old wooden card table. "Here we go!" he said cheerfully. He carefully examined the drawing Missy had made. "This should be a real snap."

Mr. Fremont took two pieces of wood and nailed each one to opposite sides of the card table, so that they were facing each other. "These are the braces for your roof," he said.

"Shouldn't they be nailed farther down?" Missy asked. "This will make the stand too top-heavy."

Mr. Fremont stood back. "Maybe you're right," he said. He pulled the nails out and repositioned the boards. Over in the corner, Baby whimpered. "No comments from you," said Mr. Fremont. He started to hammer in the first nail. "Ow!"

"Dad, be careful," Missy said, wincing.

"Nail got in the way of my finger," Mr. Fremont muttered.

Missy picked up the other hammer. "Here, Dad," she said. "Let me help you."

Two hours later Missy and her father stood back to survey their work. "Not bad," said Mr. Fremont. "What do you think?"

Missy squinted. "It looks a little lopsided," she admitted.

Mr. Fremont twisted his head to the left. "Not if you look at it this way," he said.

Missy cocked her head. "You're right, Dad." She laughed. "It looks much better this way."

Stephanie was waiting for Missy at the bus stop the next morning. "I saw you and your father building something in your garage last night," she said. "Does it have anything to do with the competition?"

"Maybe yes, maybe no," Missy answered.

"You don't have to be so secretive about it," Stephanie said.

Missy just smiled. "You'll find out soon enough," she said.

During lunch, Missy told several of the girls about her lemonade stand.

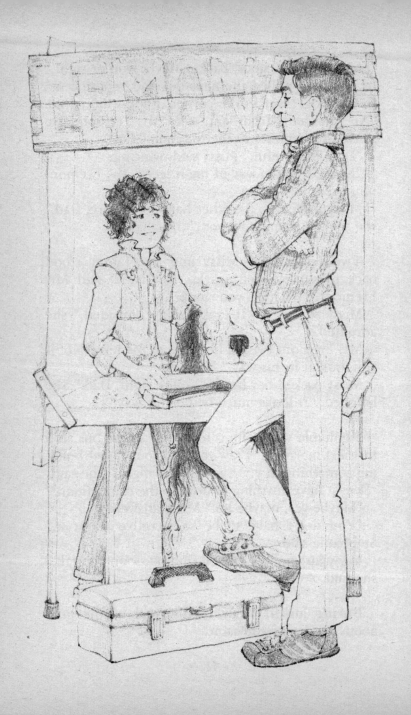

Stephanie, who was sitting at the other end of the table, overheard them talking. "A lemonade stand?" she said, making a face. "How *cute*. I had one of those when I was six."

Missy ignored Stephanie's comment.

"I wish I'd thought of a lemonade stand," sighed Ashley. "I still don't have any good ideas."

Emily nudged Missy in the ribs. "Ashley, why don't you do something with Lawrence?" she said. "I mean, he wanted you to be his partner, right?"

Ashley made a face. "That creep?" she replied. "I wouldn't be his partner for a million dollars and *twenty* trips to Washington."

"I think Lawrence likes you," Emily continued.

"No way," Ashley replied.

Willie leaned forward. "I'm going to go ask him!" she teased.

Ashley grabbed Willie's sleeve. "You'd better not," she said loudly.

"Dare me?" challenged Willie. She pulled away and ran over to the table where Lawrence and some of the other boys were sitting. The girls could see Willie talking and joking with the boys. Missy noticed Adam sitting at the table too. She wondered if he had a crush on any of the girls in their class, and if so, which girl.

Willie returned to their table with a huge grin on her face. "Guess what!" she said. "We were wrong. Lawrence *doesn't* like Ashley. He likes somebody *else*."

"Who?" asked Meredith.

"Guess," replied Willie.

The girls looked at one another. "I just hope it's not me," Christine laughed.

"Give up?" asked Willie. The girls all nodded. Willie pointed to Missy.

"Ha-ha," said Missy. "Very funny."

"I'm serious," said Willie. "See for yourself."

Missy glanced over toward Lawrence's table. He was chewing on a peanut butter sandwich and smiling at her. Missy turned green.

"Maybe he can help you with your lemonade stand," Christine said, giggling.

Missy grabbed her tray and ran to the door. "Yuck," she said. "Double yuck! Get me out of here!"

As soon as Missy got home from school, she made several pitchers of frozen lemonade.

"Do you have any piano students coming today?" Missy asked her mother. Mrs. Fremont taught beginning piano students on Saturdays and after school.

"Just two," Mrs. Fremont replied.

"Good," said Missy. "Maybe they'll buy some lemonade."

Missy dragged the lemonade stand out to the sidewalk. She hadn't even finished setting up the paper cups, when a lady with two small children pulled off the road.

"What a nice idea," squealed the lady. "It's been *ages* since I've seen a neighborhood lemonade stand. We'll take three glasses, please."

Missy used her mother's soup ladle to pour out the lemonade.

"Mmm," said the woman. "This is *very* refreshing."

"Thank you," Missy replied modestly.

Missy's next customer was Mr. Granford, who lived in the neighborhood. He asked Missy all sorts of stupid questions like whether she was trying to earn money for college and if she knew the capitals of all fifty states yet.

Business started to pick up. Both of Mrs. Fremont's piano students and several kids from the neighborhood came by. The pitchers were nearly empty. "I have to make more lemonade," Missy told Baby. She glanced across the street. Where was Stephanie? Was she hiding somewhere, just waiting for another chance to mess up Missy's business?

Missy knelt down. "I want you to guard our lemonade stand," she whispered to Baby. "Don't let *anybody* near it until I get back, okay?" Baby growled, and then wagged his tail.

Missy hurried inside. She had no sooner opened the freezer than Baby began to bark loudly. "I knew it!" Missy cried. She slammed the freezer door and ran back outside.

Stephanie was standing on top of Missy's card table, screaming. Baby had his front paws on the table and was gripping Stephanie's shoelaces with his teeth.

"I hate this dog!" Stephanie screamed.

"Baby, down," called Missy. Baby ran over to Missy and eagerly wagged his tail. "Good work," Missy whispered.

Stephanie gingerly climbed off the table. "I just

happened to be passing by, when your dog attacked me," she said with a sniff.

Missy made a sarcastic face and folded her arms across her chest. "Right, Stephanie."

"That dog has never liked me," Stephanie continued.

"You're just trying to spy on my business," accused Missy.

"You call this a business?" Stephanie hooted. She pointed to the lemonade stand. "Who built this thing anyway?"

"What's wrong with it?" Missy demanded.

"It's crooked for one thing," Stephanie replied. "It looks totally ridiculous."

"Dad and I did that on purpose," said Missy. "It gives it more character."

"You sure don't know much about carpentry, do you?" said Stephanie.

Missy's eyes narrowed.

"*My* father has a complete woodworking shop in our basement," Stephanie continued. "He would never do shabby work like this."

"You're just mad because Moose got a *real* job working in a bakery, so your car-washing business folded!" shouted Missy. "Now I've got a business and you don't."

"I am not mad," Stephanie shouted back. "And anyway, my father could make a better lemonade stand than this any day, and I'll prove it!" She shoved her hands into her jacket pockets and stalked back across the street.

"Showoff!" Missy yelled. She turned to Baby. "Great," she said. "Now what are we going to do?"

Missy's lemonade stand did a brisk business until it got dark. That evening, Baby sat next to Missy on the bed while she counted up her profits. "I'm sure I've caught up to Stephanie already," Missy said. "This was a great idea." Baby licked Missy's hand. "Thanks for all your help," Missy added. She gave him a big hug. "I don't want you to think I've forgotten about you."

Missy glanced nervously out the window. Across the street, the lights were on in Stephanie's garage, and Missy could hear a lot of hammering and sawing. Baby perked up his ears and whined. Missy scratched Baby's head. "I know," she said grimly. "I don't like it either."

CHAPTER
6

Stephanie ignored Missy at school the next day. But she told everyone *else* in the class to be sure to stop by her house after school.

"What's the big secret?" Adam asked.

"You'll see," smiled Stephanie.

At three o'clock Missy hurried home to set up her lemonade stand. Several of her classmates were already milling around Stephanie's driveway.

At three-thirty sharp Stephanie's automatic garage door opened. Baby sat up and perked his ears. Missy looked across the street and whistled. "I think we're in big trouble," she told him.

Out of Stephanie's garage rolled the most professional-looking lemonade stand Missy had ever seen. It was twice the size of Missy's, and it had a gleaming counter, painted red. Over the top of the stand was a bright red-and-white striped awning.

Stephanie carefully wheeled the lemonade stand to the end of her driveway, where it came to a graceful halt. A line formed in front of it immediately.

"No fair!" said Missy. "You're stealing my business."

"It's a free country." Stephanie shrugged.

"But there's already one lemonade stand on this block," Missy protested.

"I'm not selling lemonade," Stephanie replied indignantly. "This is a tutti-frutti punch."

A car slowed down as it drove past. "Get your fresh lemonade!" Missy shouted. "Delicious, refreshing lemonade!"

"Try my exotic tutti-frutti punch!" Stephanie called.

The man in the car rolled down his window and grinned. "Which one is better?" he asked.

"Mine," Missy and Stephanie both shouted at once.

"I use a secret recipe with six different fruit juices in it," Stephanie told him.

"Everyone just *loves* this lemonade," Missy said quickly.

The man looked at Missy's booth and then at Stephanie's booth. Stephanie flashed him her sickening-sweet smile. The red-and-white awning flapped invitingly. "I think I'll try the tutti-frutti," the man said finally.

Missy wanted to scream. Stephanie Cook, Ms. Perfect, had done it again.

"Is something the matter?" Mrs. Fremont asked her daughter during dinner. "You've hardly eaten a thing, and your mealtime conversation has been less than sparkling."

Missy shrugged. She pushed her peas around with a fork and then tried to see how many she could mash between the prongs.

"Did you have many customers today?" asked Mr. Fremont.

"None," said Missy abruptly.

Mr. and Mrs. Fremont looked at each other. "Why not?" asked Mr. Fremont.

"Stephanie's father built her this beautiful punch stand," Missy blurted out. "It even has an awning. No one wants to buy lemonade from a lopsided old card table."

Missy's father looked hurt. "There's nothing the matter with your lemonade stand," he said.

"Try telling that to the customers," Missy said glumly.

"Maybe you need a gimmick," suggested Mrs. Fremont. "Something to win your customers back."

"Like what?" Missy sighed.

"We can build something," Mr. Fremont said. "How about café tables? We'll put umbrellas in their centers and paint them white."

Mrs. Fremont raised her eyebrows. "Café tables, William?"

"Kids don't usually sit around café tables, Dad," said Missy.

"Good point," said Mr. Fremont. He scratched his head. "You know, when I was a kid, I remember there was a boy down the street who gave pony rides. He must have made a fortune."

"Where am I going to get a pony?" Missy wailed.

"Calm down, Missy," said Mrs. Fremont. "Your father's only trying to help."

"I know, Dad. I'm sorry," Missy said. She absent-mindedly rubbed her foot against Baby's paw. "I just wish I could think of a way to attract more business." Missy stopped talking and stared at Baby.

"What is it?" her father asked curiously.

Missy grinned. "Dad," she said, "do you think you could postpone your practicing again tonight? I just had a great idea and I really need your help." Missy bent down and put her arms around Baby. "And as for *you*," she whispered into Baby's ear, "I think it's time for you to start pulling your weight around here!"

7

Missy practically danced across the street to the bus stop the next morning.

"You sure are in a good mood," Tommy Lawson remarked. "Did you make a million dollars, or what?"

"Are you still planning to sell lemonade?" Stephanie asked.

"Of course," Missy replied. She smiled smugly.

When the school bus arrived, Missy flew up the steps. "Good morning, Mr. Covey," she sang. Missy ran to the back of the bus and sat down next to Emily. "Promise me you'll tell everyone you know to come by my house after school today," she said.

"What's up?" Emily wanted to know.

"You'll see," Missy answered. "Just be there, okay?"

Adam leaned forward in his seat. "Are you and Lawrence starting a hamburger stand?" he asked.

Besides peanut butter, just about the only thing Lawrence loved was hamburgers.

Missy's face turned red. "Of course not," she said. "I don't even know what Lawrence is doing for his project."

"No one does," said Tommy.

Stephanie stood up and cleared her throat. "I hope all of you can stop by *my* house later for a delicious glass of tutti-frutti punch," she said.

"What's rooti-tooti?" asked a first grader.

Everyone started to laugh. Stephanie wasn't rattled. "Aren't you cute?" she purred. "I tell you what. If you bring your mommy or daddy with you today, I'll let you try a glass for free."

The little girl smiled and clapped her hands.

Stephanie looked over at Missy to see her reaction. Missy merely shrugged. Stephanie could have all the customers she wanted today. Once they saw what Missy had planned, they'd forget about tutti-frutti punch forever.

That afternoon Missy set up her lemonade stand as usual. Then she went back into the house and waited.

A short time later Stephanie's punch stand made its appearance. Soon, there was a long line down the block.

Missy looked at Baby and smiled. "Time for our secret weapon," she said.

They went into the garage and flipped on the light. In the corner was the pony cart that she and her father had built the night before. They'd used Missy's old red wagon and some scraps of lumber to put it together.

Missy patted Baby's head. "Are you ready to be the pony?" she asked. Baby licked her hand.

Missy tied a long piece of rope to the cart and looped the other end around Baby's chest. The cart gave a creaky lurch as it slowly wobbled forward. "Perfect," said Missy. "Now for our grand entrance."

Missy opened the garage door with a flourish. "Get a free ride around the block with every glass of lemonade," she shouted, pointing to Baby's cart. Quickly, the line across the street re-formed in front of Missy's house.

Stephanie ran over. "You can't do this," she said. "You're stealing my customers!"

Missy just smiled. "Sorry, Stephanie," she replied. "It's a free country, remember?"

Word of Missy's dog cart spread quickly. By the next afternoon, the line at Missy's lemonade stand stretched halfway down the block. Some of the younger children were buying three or four glasses.

Missy was careful not to overload Baby's wagon. She didn't want to tire him out.

Across the street, Stephanie angrily flipped through the pages of a *True Romance* comic book. Denise sat miserably at her side.

Stephanie stared at the cart. "Why would anyone want to be dragged around the block in that thing?" she said loudly. "It doesn't even look safe."

"I think it looks like fun," Denise said softly.

"Oh, be quiet, Denise," snapped Stephanie. "What do you know?"

Denise picked up a dishrag and started to mop the counter top. "I'm practically a slave over here," she grumbled.

"You can leave anytime you want," said Stephanie. "I'm not stopping you."

Denise threw down her dishrag. "Good," she said. "I quit." She ran across the street and got in line.

Stephanie glared at her sister. "Traitor," she said. "I can't believe my own flesh and blood would desert me."

Denise reached into her pocket and pulled out her money. "I'd like three glasses of lemonade," she told Missy.

"That does it!" Stephanie shouted. She picked up her pitcher of tutti-frutti punch and stomped back into her house.

Denise watched her sister storm off. "Don't get too excited," she said to Missy. "She'll be back."

Ten minutes later Stephanie reappeared with a large shopping bag. "Attention, everyone," she said. She reached into the bag and pulled out a brand-new portable radio and tape deck. "I'm offering this radio to the winner of my fabulous tutti-frutti sweepstakes," she announced. Missy's customers looked up. "To enter, all you have to do is buy a glass of tutti-frutti punch," Stephanie continued.

"That's a really nice radio," said Christine. "Where did you get it?"

"My grandmother bought it for me, but I already had one," Stephanie replied. She inserted a tape and turned up the volume. "I am now open for business," she announced.

"I'm getting tired of pony rides," said a little girl. "I want to enter the sweepstakes." She walked back over to Stephanie's booth. "Me too," said her friend. One by one, Missy's customers drifted across the street.

Missy looked at Baby and sighed. "Foiled again," she said. "At this rate, I'll never win the competition!"

The next day was awful. First, Stephanie sold four raffle tickets to Adam before the school bus arrived. Then, when Missy got to the classroom, Willie sprang the next surprise.

"Hi, Missy," she mumbled.

"Willie! You got braces!" Missy exclaimed.

"Unfortunately," said Willie.

"You're so lucky," said Missy. "My parents won't let me have them." Missy wondered if Adam noticed her crooked teeth.

"Who wants braces?" said Willie. She unbent a paper clip and picked at her front tooth. "Do you know how much these things hurt?"

"But don't you get to drink a lot of milk shakes?" said Missy.

"All I've had so far is tomato soup," Willie replied.

Emily ran over. "How's your lemonade stand doing?" she asked Missy. "I'm really sorry I couldn't make it yesterday."

"Not too good," Missy replied. She told Emily and Willie all about Stephanie and her sweepstakes. Emily patted Missy sympathetically on the back. "Don't worry, you'll come up with another money-making idea."

"Right," mumbled Willie.

Emily stared at Willie. "Did you get braces?" she said.

"What does it look like?" sighed Willie.

Missy saw that Adam and Tommy were kidding around with Stephanie on the other side of the room.

"Did you hear?" Emily whispered. "Adam likes Stephanie."

Missy's face turned red. "You're kidding!" she said. No wonder Adam had bought so many raffle tickets!

"It makes perfect sense," Willie nodded. "They're the two cutest people in the class."

Missy stared at Stephanie. It was bad enough that Stephanie was stealing her business. "I don't think Stephanie is that cute," she said bluntly. "Who wants long blond hair?"

Emily shrugged. "As far as I'm concerned, they can have each other," she said. "They're both stuck-up."

Missy took her seat and pretended to study her math textbook. How could Adam like Stephanie? Couldn't he see what a creep she was? Missy looked up and glanced across the room where Adam's seat was. She saw that Lawrence was staring at her again. Missy made a face at him.

"Quit bothering me, Lawrence," she muttered under her breath. "Can't you see I'm not interested?"

*   *   *

Later that evening Missy stood in front of her bathroom mirror and frowned. "I need a new look," she said aloud.

"There's nothing wrong with your appearance," said Mrs. Fremont as she walked past the door.

"To start with," Missy stated, "my teeth are crooked."

Mrs. Fremont laughed. "Hardly," she said.

Missy shook her shaggy mane of hair impatiently. "I could also use a more mature hair style," she told her mother. "I've worn my hair like this since the first grade."

"That's true," admitted her mother. "What kind of hair style did you have in mind?"

"Oh, nothing drastic," Missy replied. "Maybe just a few blond streaks to start with."

"I don't think I've ever seen a redhead with blond streaks," said Mrs. Fremont.

"Maybe you're right," said Missy. "I don't want to overdo it." She sighed loudly. "I just wish my hair wasn't so curly."

"Curly hair is very popular now," said Mrs. Fremont.

"Not in my class," said Missy. "The most popular girls all have straight hair."

"When I was your age, I used to iron my hair to get the curls out," laughed Mrs. Fremont.

"Did it work?" asked Missy.

"Well . . . sort of," her mother replied. She looked at her daughter and smiled. "How's the lemonade stand working out?" she asked.

"I've decided to try another business," Missy replied. "The competition was getting too heavy."

"What's your new business going to be?" Mrs. Fremont wanted to know.

"Baby and I were thinking of taking the dog cart over to Sherman's Supermarket," Missy told her. "We can take people's groceries from the store to their cars."

"A grocery delivery service!" said Mrs. Fremont. "What a great idea."

Missy looked in the mirror and frowned. "I sure hope so," she said. "It's about time my luck changed."

CHAPTER

8

The next afternoon Missy and Baby stood outside Sherman's and shared a bag of potato chips. When they were finished, Missy brushed the crumbs away from her mouth and looked down at Baby. "Are we ready for business?" she asked him. Baby barked and licked her hand.

A woman with a small child and her arms full of groceries came walking out of the automatic doors. "Need help with those groceries, ma'am?" asked Missy.

The woman looked at her and smiled. "Are you for hire?" she asked.

Missy nodded and named her price.

"Horsie." The little girl pointed at Baby.

"Would you like to ride with the groceries?" Missy asked her. The little girl squealed and clapped her hands. Missy helped her climb into the wagon.

Then she loaded the wagon with the groceries and took off across the parking lot.

"Wheee," said the little girl, grabbing hold of Baby's fur. "Fun!"

"No, no," said Missy. Baby gave a little growl and stopped short, right in the middle of the parking lot. Missy quickly removed the little girl's hands, but Baby still wouldn't budge.

"Come *on*, Baby," Missy hissed. "You can't stop here. We'll get run over!"

Baby looked up at Missy and whined.

"*Please*, Baby, do it for me," begged Missy. "I promise you she won't pull your fur again." She gave Baby a little push. He started to move forward slowly, and Missy breathed a sigh of relief.

Missy carefully lifted the woman's groceries into the trunk of her car. The little girl had managed to climb out of the wagon by herself. "Thanks so much," said the woman as she paid Missy.

Missy returned to the front of the store, where another woman with two small children and a load of groceries was already waiting. "Are you *sure* your dog doesn't mind pulling the kids too?" the woman asked.

"Not at all," Missy replied. She noticed Baby's ears flatten. "Baby, these kids aren't that heavy," she whispered. "Besides, it's a good way to get more business."

Missy squeezed the five bags of groceries and the two children into the cart.

"Giddy up," shouted one of the boys. He stood up and hung on to Baby's back. Baby growled a little louder this time.

"Leave the doggie alone and sit *down,* Sammy," said the boy's mother sharply. Sammy sat down.

Missy hurried across the parking lot and unloaded everything as quickly as she could. Baby put his tail between his legs and headed back to the automatic doors.

"What's the matter?" Missy asked. "You never used to mind this."

As the afternoon wore on, Baby got slower and slower. "We're never going to win the competition if you continue to walk like a turtle," Missy complained.

Baby looked the other way and pretended not to hear her.

"Excuse me," said a tall man. He pointed to the lumber store on the other side of Sherman's. "Would you be willing to help me carry some lumber to my car? I think it's going to take about three trips and I'll be happy to pay you extra."

"Sure," said Missy. She tugged lightly on Baby's collar. "Let's go."

Baby didn't budge.

Missy looked at the man and smiled. "We'll be there in just a minute," she said. She knelt down. "I know what you're doing and I don't like it," she whispered into Baby's ear.

Baby sat down.

"Stop it!" said Missy. "You're embarrassing me!" She gave Baby's collar a strong tug.

"Looks like your dog has gone on strike," commented the man. He looked at his watch.

"We'll be with you and your lumber in no time."

Missy puffed as she continued to tug on Baby's collar.

"Never mind, I'll do it myself," he replied. "I really need to get going."

Missy gave Baby a strong push from behind. He gave a low, angry growl. Missy hopped out of the way. "Okay, okay," she said quickly. "I get the message." She undid the rope around his chest. "I can see it's pointless to try to force you to do this," she told him. "Let's go home."

That evening, Missy was sitting on her bed, trying to figure out her profits, when the phone rang.

"It's Willie," called Mrs. Fremont.

"How's it going, Willie?" asked Missy.

"I'm having a lot of trouble earning enough money in this stupid competition," Willie replied. "Not that many people want to have their nails manicured."

"Maybe you're not 'handy' enough," joked Missy.

"Very funny," muttered Willie. "Anyway, I was talking to Emily and some of the other girls, and we thought it would be fun to do something together. We can split whatever profits we make."

"What did you have in mind?"

"A bake sale," Willie replied. "Interested?"

Missy looked over at Baby. "I guess so," she sighed. "I mean, my dog wash was a flop, my lemonade business folded, and Baby is being a totally uncooperative delivery dog."

Baby lifted his head and whimpered.

"I'm ready to try anything at this point," Missy added.

"Good," said Willie approvingly. "Tomorrow night we're all going to Stephanie's for a sleep-over. We can do our baking at her house."

"A sleep-over at Stephanie's?" said Missy. Her throat started to feel tight.

"I've gotta go," said Willie. "My brother wants to use the phone." She hung up.

Missy replaced the receiver and made a face. "Yuck," she said. "The last place on earth I want to be is at Stephanie's house." Missy sighed. "Oh, well. I guess it won't be so bad if all the other girls are there. Besides," she added, "what else can Stephanie do to me that she hasn't done already?"

CHAPTER

9

"**M**issy," called her mother the next morning, "where are you?"

"In the basement," Missy yelled.

"You'd better hurry up," shouted Mrs. Fremont. "I can see the school bus coming."

Missy put down the iron. "But I'm not ready yet," she said frantically. "Only half my hair is ironed." She glanced in an old dresser mirror that hung in the corner. "This looks horrible!" she gasped.

"I can't hear you," Mrs. Fremont called from upstairs. "Is something the matter?"

Missy quickly snatched her father's favorite baseball cap off the top of the washing machine and shoved her hair underneath it. "Coming, Mom," she yelled. She clattered up the steps.

"You aren't wearing that old hat to school, are you?" asked Mrs. Fremont.

Missy grabbed her book bag and raced out the door. "It's okay, Mom," she said. "This is an emergency. I'll explain later."

Missy flipped back the bill of the cap and ran. "Wait for me, Mr. Covey," she yelled. She made it to the bus just in time.

Missy walked to the back and sat down next to Emily. Adam turned around in his seat.

"Where's your hair?" he asked.

Missy turned bright red. "Under my hat," she said. "Where else would it be?"

"It's probably just dirty," sniffed Stephanie.

"It is not!" said Missy. She pulled the hat down as far as it would go and then folded her arms in front of her chest. The first thing she was going to do when she got to school was wet down her hair in the girls' bathroom.

"Are you going to Stephanie's tonight?" Emily asked in a low voice.

"I guess so." Missy shrugged.

"What recipe are you bringing?" said Emily.

"My grandmother's brownie recipe," Missy replied. She watched Stephanie open a bag of potato chips and offer one to Adam.

Emily nudged Missy in the ribs. "What did I tell you?" she whispered. She drew the shape of a heart in the air.

Missy felt slightly sick to her stomach. "I think I need some air," she said. As she reached across Emily and opened the window, a huge gust of wind blew through the bus.

"Missy!" gasped Emily. "Your hat!"

Missy's hat flew out the window and bounced

across the road. Missy quickly ducked down, pulled her jacket over her head, and prayed that no one had seen her hair.

"Hey, Missy," shouted Adam. "Did your head get flattened out by a truck?"

Missy thought she was going to die of embarrassment.

Ashley bent forward and gave Missy her most concerned expression. "You don't look too good," she said in her nasal voice. "Did you know one side of your hair is all matted down?"

"See? I told you it was dirty," said Stephanie smugly.

"Would everyone please just leave me alone?" begged Missy. "There's nothing the matter with my hair. I just slept on it wrong."

Stephanie finished her potato chips and daintily wiped her mouth with a napkin. "You wouldn't have that problem," she said, "if you washed it every morning, like *I* do."

"Thanks, Stephanie," Missy muttered. "Thanks a *lot*."

When Missy got home that afternoon, Mrs. Fremont was in the kitchen stacking the egg cartons that she'd been collecting all winter. She was going to use them to plant seedlings with her kindergarten class.

Missy flopped down on the floor next to Baby and buried her face in his fur. "Nothing seems to be going my way lately," she sighed.

"Tough day?" asked her mother.

"To begin with, I lost Dad's baseball cap," Missy

said. "It flew off my head while I was on the bus this morning."

"Dad's not going to be too pleased to hear that," said Mrs. Fremont.

"I also got a tardy slip," Missy continued. "I was late to class because I was in the bathroom wetting down my hair." Mrs. Fremont looked puzzled. "I tried to iron it, but it didn't exactly work," Missy explained.

"Bad suggestion," said Mrs. Fremont. "Sorry."

"I've also changed my mind about wanting braces," Missy added. "Lawrence Shoemaker just got them. I've never been so grossed out in my life."

She grabbed Baby around the neck and hugged him. Baby gave a low growl.

Missy threw up her hands. "Don't tell me *you're* against me, too," she said. She lay on her back and looked up at the kitchen ceiling. "I've decided not to go to Stephanie's sleep-over tonight," she said. "Stephanie and I both had brownie recipes, and the girls voted to make hers instead of mine."

"That's too bad," said Mrs. Fremont. "Your grandmother's brownies are the world's greatest."

"No one would listen to me," Missy said. "Can't I stay home and watch TV instead?"

Mrs. Fremont shook her head. "Sorry, dear, we're going out. Besides, I'm sure that if you give it a chance, you'll have a great time."

"Great time?" Missy moaned. "This is *Stephanie's* house, remember?"

Missy anxiously bit her lower lip as she rang Stephanie's bell. She could hear all the girls laughing inside.

Stephanie opened the door with a big phony smile. When she saw it was Missy, her face fell. "Oh, it's just you," she said. "You might as well come in."

"Who were you expecting?" asked Missy as she marched through the door. "A movie star?"

"Some of the boys said they might come over," Stephanie replied.

"Probably Adam," Missy thought. She wasn't sure if she could stand the sight of Stephanie and Adam together—Stephanie acted even *more* sickening than usual when she was around Adam.

The girls were all downstairs in Stephanie's family room practicing cheers. "Hi, Missy," shouted Willie. Missy noticed that Willie had already changed into her pajamas. She was wearing an old baggy college T-shirt that said INDIANA STATE IS GREAT!

"Hey, you guys, shouldn't we be up in the kitchen, baking?" Meredith asked. "We haven't got all night, you know!" She and Christine were in charge of the recipes.

"I want to change into my nightgown first," said Amy. "Me too," echoed Kate Richardson.

"But what if the boys come over?" interrupted Emily.

"I don't think they're coming," said Stephanie. "They would have been here by now."

Missy had brought her favorite nightgown, the one with tiny pink and purple flowers. She quickly undressed and put it on. Then she ran upstairs to the kitchen.

Mrs. Cook was walking around the kitchen looking nervous. This was the first time she'd had so many girls spend the night, and she didn't want her kitchen to be totally destroyed.

"Emily, catch," said Willie. A bag of flour came flying across the room.

Emily lunged for the bag and missed. The bag split open, dumping flour all over the floor. Mrs. Cook closed her eyes and looked like she was going to faint. "Sorry, Mrs. Cook," Emily said. "I'll clean it up."

Mrs. Cook pressed a hand to her forehead. "That's all right, dear," she replied weakly. "I'll be upstairs if anyone needs anything." She quickly disappeared.

It was a good thing Stephanie's mother wasn't on hand, because by nine o'clock the Cooks' kitchen looked like a battle zone. Mixing bowls and pans were strewn across the counters. In the middle of the kitchen table sat several cakes, a plate of cookies, and Stephanie's gourmet brownies, which she had decided to frost with strawberry icing.

Stephanie was sitting at the head of the table, licking the last bit of frosting out of the bowl. "I predict," she said, "that these brownies will be the first thing to sell out."

Missy looked at Emily and rolled her eyes. Stephanie had been bragging about her brownies all evening.

"Now what?" asked Kate as she surveyed the scene.

"Why don't we go downstairs and listen to music," suggested Amy. Naturally, Stephanie had every good CD in the world.

"I think we'd better clean up first," said Chris-

tine. The girls nodded in unison and quickly got to work.

After every pot and pan had been scrubbed, and the counter tops and floor had been washed, Willie tossed her dish towel in the air and gave a loud whoop. "I quit!" she shouted gleefully.

"Shh," cautioned Ashley. "There are other people in this house, Willie."

Willie made a face at her and headed for the family room. "Let's go call some of the boys," she said.

"Are you crazy?" said Christine, raising her eyebrows.

Willie raced downstairs and dialed the phone. "May I speak with Adam?" she said.

Missy watched Willie enviously. She would never have the courage to pick up the phone and call *Adam*.

"Hi, Adam," said Willie. "What's happening?" All the girls pressed closer.

Suddenly, Stephanie snatched the phone from Willie. "Let me talk to him," she said. Stephanie got on the line. "I thought you and Tommy were coming over," she said. Stephanie looked around at the girls and smiled. She listened for a moment and then nodded. "See you soon," she said.

After Stephanie hung up the phone, everyone began talking at once. "What did they say?" asked Meredith.

"Are they really coming over?" added Amy.

"Maybe," said Stephanie mysteriously.

"But we're all in our pajamas," said Emily.

"That's okay," said Stephanie. "We'll just talk to

them through the window. My parents won't let boys come over this late anyway."

The girls rushed upstairs and peeked out the living-room curtains. "I think I see them!" said Kate.

"Where?" said Christine. Everyone crowded around the window.

Suddenly Stephanie got a funny look on her face. "I'm going to look for them out the front door," she said. "Come help me, Missy."

Missy followed her suspiciously. "Why does Stephanie need help just to look out the door?" she wondered.

Stephanie opened the door and peered out. "Look! Over there! I think that's them." She pointed.

As Missy leaned forward, she suddenly felt herself being pushed out the door. "Ow!" she said. She turned around just in time to see Stephanie grinning as she slammed the front door shut and locked it. Missy couldn't believe it! Stephanie had locked her outside in her nightgown! She pounded on the door. "Let me in!" she shouted. Of all the sneaky tricks Stephanie had pulled on Missy, this was the worst!

Missy suddenly stiffened. She could hear laughing and talking. The voices got louder. The boys were almost at the house! Missy realized frantically. She had to get out of there fast! Missy quickly ducked down, crawled off the front porch, and hid behind the nearest bush. Had the boys seen her?

Adam and Tommy walked up to the front steps. Missy flattened herself against the bush. She could see Adam and Tommy talking to Stephanie and the other girls through the living-room window. Several cars drove past. How in the world was she ever going to get out of there without anyone seeing her?

Something soft and furry came bounding up to brush against Missy. "Baby!" she said softly. "Am I glad to see you!"

Baby sniffed Missy's face and wagged his tail.

"I need your help," she whispered. She looked over at the window. Everyone was still busy talking and joking together.

Missy bent down and grabbed hold of Baby's coat. "You'll have to hide me," she said. Keeping one eye on the living-room window, Missy crept out of the bushes and safely past Adam and Tommy.

Missy didn't remember her parents were out until she reached the doorstep. "Oh, great," she said. "Locked out of my own house too." She wrapped her arms around her chest and shivered. Even though it was late spring, the night air was chilly.

Baby licked her hand and whimpered. Missy looked down at him. "I don't suppose you could make a little room for me in your doghouse," she said. Baby barked softly.

Soon Missy and Baby were huddled inside the doghouse. Missy put her head against Baby's warm coat. She could still hear Tommy's and Adam's voices over in Stephanie's yard. It sounded as though they were having a great time.

Missy gazed out the door at Stephanie's brightly lit house and wished for a cup of hot chocolate. She

wondered how Stephanie had explained her sudden "disappearance." Probably no one had even noticed that she was missing. Missy shivered again and moved closer to Baby. "Stephanie Cook," she said softly, "I'll get even with you if it's the last thing I do!"

CHAPTER
10

_____

"**W**hat happened to you last night?" Emily asked Missy the next morning. "Stephanie said you were feeling sick and went home."

Missy looked at Stephanie, who was bragging about her brownies to Adam, and shrugged. "You could say that," she replied. She didn't want to give Stephanie the pleasure of knowing that she'd succeeded in humiliating her.

"You missed the boys," Emily added.

"I know." Missy nodded. She thought about how her parents had found her sound asleep in Baby's doghouse. Boy, were they angry!

"You're still going to help with the bake sale after school, aren't you?" asked Emily.

"Of course," Missy replied. "I'm bringing the card tables, remember?" Missy looked at Stephanie again and smiled. It was time to put her plan into action.

"Do you think anyone will mind if I bring Baby?" she said casually. "He loves bake sales."

Emily shook her head. "Of course not. Everyone loves having Baby around."

"Good." Missy nodded. She calmly sat down and opened her social studies book. There was no reason why anyone should suspect a thing.

After school, Missy took the bus home. Her mother had agreed to drive her back with the tables—and Baby.

"Are you sure you want to use these old card tables?" said Mrs. Fremont as she helped Missy load them into the car. "They don't look very sturdy to me."

"Believe me, Mom," smiled Missy, "they're perfect, absolutely perfect."

Baby wagged his tail from the back seat.

When Missy and Baby got to school, the girls were already busy setting things up in the cafeteria. Christine and Meredith were putting price stickers on everything, and Amy was organizing the cash box.

Stephanie glared when she saw what Missy was wearing for the sale. "That's *my* sweater!" she said.

Missy smiled at her. "Now it's my sweater since *I* had to pay for it." The look on Stephanie's face was worth all the money she still owed her mother.

Stephanie pointed angrily at Baby. "And what's he doing here?" she snapped. "We can't have a dog at the sale. It's a health hazard."

Missy remained calm. "Don't worry," she said pleasantly. "I'll take him outside as soon as the sale starts." She smiled again at Stephanie and started to set up the card tables.

Stephanie grabbed one of the tables and dragged it over near the door. "I think my brownies should have their own table," she announced.

Missy acted surprised. Her plan was working perfectly. "They should?" she asked innocently.

"They're a gourmet item," Stephanie said. "They also cost more."

Missy frowned. "I don't think we have enough card tables."

Stephanie placed her brownies on the table. "Trust me," she said firmly.

"If you say so." Missy shrugged.

Soon the cafeteria was ready. Ashley ran over and peeked out the door. "There are about a hundred kids out here!" she shouted. "Is it time to open up?"

Missy took a deep breath. "I have to get something out of the classroom first," she said. She turned to Stephanie. "Would you mind if I tied Baby to your table for one minute?"

Before Stephanie had a chance to answer, Missy looped Baby's leash around the table leg. "I'll be back in a flash," she said. She hurried out of the cafeteria and ducked into the girls' bathroom.

Missy stood by the bathroom sink and counted to sixty five times. "By now," Missy thought, "Baby should be getting restless."

Soon Missy heard a lot of commotion in the cafeteria. "That's him," she said. "Right on schedule." She walked back into the hallway, whistling softly.

Just then Baby came tearing down the hall still tied to the card table. Across the cafeteria and down the hall lay a gooey trail of chocolate brownies and strawberry icing.

"Stop him," yelled Stephanie.

Missy grabbed Baby. Then she knelt down and untangled his leash. "I'm sorry," she told Stephanie innocently. "I forgot how restless Baby gets whenever he's tied up for too long."

Stephanie's face turned purple. "You did that on purpose," she sputtered.

Missy's eyebrows lifted. "Who, me?" she said.

A crowd of students was gathering around the two girls and Baby. Just then, Ms. Van Sickel marched up to them. "Girls," she said. "What is going on here?"

Stephanie pointed a finger at Missy. "She deliberately ruined my brownies," she said.

Ms. Van Sickel looked at Missy. "Is that true?" she asked.

Now it was Missy's turn to get angry. "Only because she locked me out of her house during our sleep-over!" she replied. "And I was in my nightgown!"

Emily and Willie gasped in disbelief. "But Stephanie told us you got sick," they both said at the same time.

Stephanie made a face. "She stole my customers," she said.

"What about the hole in my garden hose?" Missy interrupted.

Ms. Van Sickel clapped her hands. "Girls!" she cried. "I'm surprised at you both. This was supposed to be a friendly competition."

"Not with Stephanie around," Missy grumbled.

Everyone began talking at once. Ms. Van Sickel clapped her hands again. "It seems that you two have forgotten the purpose of the competition," she said. "We were trying to earn money for a class trip, not participate in property destruction." She looked sternly at the gathered students. "The contest is over," she told them. "Please bring in whatever money you've earned tomorrow." She turned on her heel and walked away angrily.

Missy felt terrible. She knew she had disappointed Ms. Van Sickel and her classmates. The bake sale had turned into a disaster, thanks to her. But she was still angry with Stephanie. She wanted to win now more than ever. "The contest may be over, Stephanie," she said, "but I'm still going to end up the winner."

Stephanie glared back at her. "Don't be so sure," she snapped.

That evening Missy sat in her bedroom and anxiously counted up her profits. Sixty-five dollars suddenly didn't seem like that much.

There was a knock at the door.

"Come in," Missy called.

Mr. Fremont entered and sat down on the bed. "Look at all the loot!" He grinned. "Looks like you've been spending your Saturdays holding up gas stations."

"Banks," said Missy with a straight face. "Baby was my accomplice. He pulled the getaway cart."

"Aha," said her father. "Now the truth comes out!" He looked at Missy and paused. "Your mother and I just got a phone call from Ms. Van Sickel," he said. "She didn't sound too pleased."

Missy twisted the corner of the bedspread around her finger. "What did she say?" she asked.

"She was surprised by your behavior at the bake sale today," he replied quietly. He paused again. "Frankly, so was I."

"It isn't my fault," said Missy. "Blame Ms. Perfect, Stephanie Cook."

"Why do you say that?" asked her father.

"Everything about Stephanie is perfect," Missy replied glumly. "Perfect hair, perfect clothes, perfect teeth. She always has to have her own way too. It's not fair. Other people deserve a chance."

"I agree." Her father nodded. "But do you think that someone who would deliberately put a hole in your garden hose is perfect?"

"I didn't say her behavior was perfect," Missy said. "And anyway, no one seems to care about her behavior."

"Ms. Van Sickel certainly does," said her father. "She was planning to call Stephanie's parents next. And what's more important anyway?" he added. "Winning or doing your best?"

Missy thought about what her father said. Maybe he had a point. Maybe she *had* carried this competition a little too far. She reached over and gave him a hug. "You know what I like most about you, Dad?" she said.

"My carpentry skills?" he replied hopefully.

Missy laughed. "Whenever we have a talk, I always feel like I've learned something."

Mr. Fremont squeezed his daughter's hand. "That's probably because you knew it all along," he said.

"But what I *still* don't know," thought Missy, "is who the winner of the competition will be."

CHAPTER 11

Ms. Van Sickel stood in front of the blackboard and cleared her throat. "All right, class," she said, "when I read your name, I'd like each of you to call out the amount you're contributing to the trip."

Missy glanced nervously around the room. Despite everything, she still wanted to beat Stephanie, just this once.

"David Holt," said Ms. Van Sickel.

"Fifty dollars," he said. Everyone gave an appreciative murmur. Ms. Van Sickel looked pleased.

"Ashley Woods." Ashley had managed to sell off some of her old CDs.

"Nine fifty," she said. Ms. Van Sickel nodded and wrote the amount on the blackboard.

As Ms. Van Sickel continued down the list, the butterflies in Missy's stomach got worse. When would the teacher get to her and Stephanie? Finally, she heard Ms. Van Sickel call her name.

Missy took a deep breath. "Sixty-five dollars," she announced.

"I believe that's our highest figure yet," said Ms. Van Sickel as she wrote it down on the blackboard.

Missy peeked at Stephanie, who was sitting next to her. Very casually, Stephanie reached into her desk, pulled three dollars out of her wallet, and added it to the cash envelope on her desk!

"Stephanie?" said Ms. Van Sickel. "How much did you raise?"

Stephanie held up her envelope. "Sixty-six dollars!" she said triumphantly.

Missy couldn't believe it! She had won, fair and square, and Stephanie was cheating her out of her victory. Missy's hand shot up angrily. "Ms. Van Sickel," she said. "I have something to say."

"Let's finish this first," Ms. Van Sickel replied. "Who haven't I called on?"

Lawrence Shoemaker raised his hand.

"How much were you able to earn?" said Ms. Van Sickel with a smile.

Lawrence pulled a large paper bag out of his desk. "One fifty," he said.

"One dollar and fifty cents?" asked Ms. Van Sickel. The class tittered.

Lawrence shook his head. "One hundred and fifty dollars," he said.

Ms. Van Sickel put down her piece of chalk and stared at him. "Are you sure that figure is correct?" she asked.

Lawrence reached into the paper bag and pulled

out a fistful of dollar bills. "I may be a dollar or two off," he admitted. "It's hard to count all of these ones."

Missy's eyes widened. She'd never seen that much money in her life.

Ms. Van Sickel cleared her throat. "Lawrence," she said, "how in the world did you earn that much money?"

Lawrence proudly held up a copy of *The Indianapolis Gazette*. "I ran an ad in the newspaper every day for three weeks," he said. "It was kind of expensive, but it was worth it." Ms. Van Sickel looked confused. Lawrence brought the newspaper to the front of the room and pointed to the classified ad section in the back.

" 'Turn ordinary hamburgers into gourmet delights with 101 hamburger recipes,' " read Ms. Van Sickel proudly. " 'Send $1.50 to L. Shoemaker, P.O. Box 88159, Indpls., Ind. 46208.' "

"We were swamped," Lawrence admitted. He showed the class a small photocopied booklet that said *Hamburgers, Hamburgers, Hamburgers!* on the front. "This was what I sent people after I received their money," he explained.

Missy was impressed.

"Where did you get the recipes?" asked Willie.

"Mom and I made them up," Lawrence replied. "We tested every single one." He rolled his eyes and held his stomach.

The whole class laughed. "Well!" said Ms. Van Sickel. "It looks as if Lawrence has almost financed our whole trip single-handedly. Very good work."

Lawrence smiled modestly and took his seat again.

Ms. Van Sickel turned to Missy. "Now, what was it you wanted to say?" she asked pleasantly.

Missy looked directly at Stephanie. Stephanie instinctively reached out and put her hand on her cash envelope. "Never mind," said Missy. "It wasn't important."

After class most of the students ran over to Lawrence's desk to look at his bag of money before Ms. Van Sickel took it to the school safe. Emily even bought one of his recipe books.

Missy walked over to Stephanie's desk. "Looks like we both lost, Stephanie," she said.

"What are you talking about?" Stephanie replied haughtily.

Missy shrugged and said, "Come on, Stephanie. I'm willing to admit *I* lost. Why can't you?"

Stephanie quickly grabbed Missy's arm. "I'll give you ten dollars if you won't tell on me," she said.

"I'm not going to tell that you cheated," Missy answered. "And I don't want your money."

"Well, what *do* you want?" Stephanie asked suspiciously.

"I told you what I wanted," Missy said. "Once, just once, I want to hear you admit that you lost."

"All right." Stephanie glared at Missy. "*I lost*. Now are you happy?"

"To tell you the truth, I feel kind of stupid," Missy admitted, "fighting so hard with you to win the contest, and then losing to *Lawrence*."

Stephanie began to laugh. "I know what you mean," she said. "I felt so dumb. Especially after slipping in that extra money . . ." She stopped laughing. "Look, I'm sorry, Missy."

Missy looked at her for a moment. "How about a truce between you and me?" she finally said. "No more arguments, no more insults, no more sneaky tricks. What do you say?"

Stephanie was silent, then she nodded her head. "I suppose we can give it a try," she said grudgingly. "After all, we *do* live across the street from each other." She gave Missy a little smile. "Unfortunately."

Missy smiled back. She suspected that Stephanie would never *really* change. But getting her to agree to a truce was a step in the right direction. Missy's smile grew broader. She may not have won the competition. But she was beginning to feel like a real winner just the same.